HELLO, I'M THEA!

I'm *Geronimo Stilton*'s sister. As I'm sure you know from my brother's bestselling novels, I'm a special correspondent for *The Rodent's Gazette*, Mouse Island's most famous newspaper. Unlike my 'fraidy mouse brother, I absolutely adore traveling, having adventures, and meeting rodents from all around the world!

The adventure I want to tell you about begins at Mouseford Academy, the school I went to when I was a young mouseling. I had such a great experience there as a student that I came back to teach a journalism class.

When I returned as a grown mouse, I met five really special students: Colette, Nicky, Pamela, Paulina, and Violet. You could hardly imagine five more different mouselings, but they became great friends right away. And they liked me so much that they decided to name their group after me: the Thea Sisters! I was so touched by that, I decided to write about their adventures. So turn the page to read a fabumouse adventure about the

THEA SISTERS!

Colette

She has a passion for clothing and style, especially anything pink. When she grows up, she wants to be a fashion editor.

Paulina

Cheerful and kind, she loves traveling and meeting rodents from all over the world. She has a magic touch when it comes to technology.

Violet

She's the bookworm of the group, and she loves learning. She enjoys classical music and dreams of becoming a famouse violinist.

THE THEA SISTERS

Nicky

She comes from Australia and is very enthusiastic about sports and nature. She loves being outside and is always ready to get up and go!

Pamela

She is a great mechanic: Give her a screwdriver and she'll fix anything! She loves pizza, which she eats every day, and she loves to cook.

Do you want to help the Thea Sisters in this new adventure? It's not hard — just follow the clues!

When you see this magnifying glass, pay attention: It means there's an important clue on the page. Each time one appears, we'll review the clues so we don't miss anything.

**ARE YOU READY?
A NEW MYSTERY AWAITS!**

Thea Stilton

THEA STILTON AND THE **ROMAN** HOLIDAY

Scholastic Inc.

Copyright © 2017 Edizioni Piemme S.p.A. © 2018 Mondadori Libri S.p.A. for PIEMME, Italia, Italy. International Rights © Atlantyca S.p.A., Via Leopardi 8, 20123 Milan, Italy; foreignrights@atlantyca.it, atlantyca.com English translation © 2021 by Atlantyca S.p.A.

The publisher does not have any control over and does not assume any responsibility for author or third-party websites or their content.

GERONIMO STILTON and THEA STILTON names, characters, and related indicia are copyright, trademark, and exclusive license of Atlantyca S.p.A. All rights reserved. The moral right of the author has been asserted. Based on an original idea by Elisabetta Dami. geronimostilton.com.

Published by Scholastic Inc., *Publishers since 1920*, 557 Broadway, New York, NY 10012. SCHOLASTIC and associated logos are trademarks and/or registered trademarks of Scholastic Inc.

Stilton is the name of a famous English cheese. It is a registered trademark of the Stilton Cheese Makers' Association. For more information, go to stiltoncheese.com.

ISBN 978-1-338-75687-6

Text by Thea Stilton
Original title *Caccia al Tesoro a Roma*
Art director: Iacopo Bruno
Cover by Valeria Brambilla and Flavio Ferron
Illustrations by Valeria Brambilla, Barbara Pellizzari, Valeria Cairoli, Valentina Grassini, and Flavio Ferron
Graphics by Chiara Cebraro

Special thanks to AnnMarie Anderson
Translated by Julia Heim
Interior design by Kay Petronio

10 9 8 7 6 5 4 3 2 1   21 22 23 24 25

Printed in the U.S.A.   40
First printing 2021

FiNAL
PREPARATiONS

It was a beautiful day at Mouseford Academy, and one room in the dorm was *buzzing* with activity.

"**PAM!**" a voice squeaked from inside a closet. "Where's my straw hat with the pink-polka-dotted turquoise ribbon?"

A second later, Colette emerged from behind a rack of dresses. She scampered over to the bed and rummaged through an ENORMOUSE pile of clothes and accessories.

"How should I know, Coco?" Pam replied with a shrug. "There must be around fifty hats here, but I don't see that one anywhere."

"*At least I found these!*" Colette said. She pulled out a pair of **PINK** sandals from under a pile of handbags. "I simply have to bring them!"

At that moment Nicky, Violet, and Paulina appeared in the doorway.

"Are you two ready?" Nicky asked as she looked around the room. "Whoa! What happened in here? **Did a hurricane hit?!**"

"It's just our Coco," Pam said with a laugh. "She's trying to pack her **bags**. I told her we would only be away for a week, but you know Colette."

"I don't care how long we're staying," Colette protested. "What matters is that we're going to **Italy**, a country where fashion and elegance are very important! I need to be prepared for any occasion!"

"Yes, but we're going to **Rome** for an archaeology competition, not a fashion show!" Violet pointed out.

A few days earlier, the Thea Sisters had learned they had been chosen to participate in

the **International Archaeology Games** being held in Rome, Italy. A month before that, Amalia Angel, a famouse Italian researcher, had been invited to Mouseford to give an *INTENSIVE* seminar on Roman archaeology.

The five friends had signed up for the seminar **IMMEDIATELY**, and after just a few classes, they were hooked on archaeology! Professor Angel gave fascinating lectures about life in **ancient Rome**. The Thea Sisters

THE COLOSSEUM

loved her stories about the incredible **works of art** that were created during that time period.

"I know, but I still need to look **fabumouse**," Colette replied as she tried to close her suitcase without much success.

"Do you remember how much research we did on ancient **ROMAN** buildings like the Colosseum?" Paulina asked.

"It took a long time, but it was **WORTH IT!**" Violet squeaked. "Thanks to that research, Professor Angel nominated us for the competition. I feel like the **LUCKIEST** mouse in the world right now!"

"I know!" Colette agreed as she sat on her bag to get it to **CLOSE**. "I was so surprised when our acceptance letter arrived."

"And just think, we leave today!" Nicky exclaimed. She leaned over Colette and snapped the lock on her friend's bag shut.

"Thanks!" Colette squeaked with a sigh of relief. "Four more bags and I'll be all set! I just need to find one last thing . . ."

"What's this doing here?" Paulina asked as she **PULLED** something out from behind the chair cushion.

Here's our research!

"That's my **straw hat**!" Colette exclaimed. "Way to go, Paulina. You found it!"

"Great!" Pam said, hopping up from the chair. "Now I think we're ready to go.

ROME IS WAITING!"

ANCIENT ROME

According to ancient mythology, **Rome was founded in 753 BC** by Romulus, who was raised by a wolf along with his twin brother, Remus. Today, the Capitoline Wolf — a bronze sculpture depicting the founding of Rome — is considered a symbol of the city.

Rome was governed for more than two hundred years by seven kings: **Romulus, Numa Pompilius, Tullus Hostilius, Ancus Marcius, Lucius Tarquinius Priscus, Servius Tullius, and Lucius Tarquinius Superbus.** Once the republic of Rome was founded, it lasted for five hundred years, and Rome became the capital of an enormous empire that stretched across a large part of modern Europe, part of Africa, and part of Asia.

The Roman Empire reached the height of its splendor in the first centuries AD. The western half of the empire declined quickly, while the eastern half of the Roman Empire (later known as the Byzantine Empire) survived until 1453.

DRAMA IN THE AIR

"I don't know about the rest of you, but I can't wait to get to **Rome**!" Nicky told her friends as they boarded their flight.

"Think of how **great** it will be," Violet said dreamily. "We're going to spend a week in one of the most fascinating cities in the world."

What a stupendous city!

"It's going to be unforgettable," Colette agreed as she slipped into the seat next to them.

"This is UNACCEPTABLE!" came a sudden, sharp squeak behind the Thea Sisters.

"I can only travel if I'm sitting by the window. Here I'll be squished between two seats."

"I'm sorry, but the seats are assigned **electronically**," the flight attendant explained kindly.

"I already agreed to travel in economy," the mouselet continued. "But this is just TOO MUCH!"

"Mélanie, would you like to change seats?" the mouse sitting next to the window asked timidly.

"Oh, all right," the mouse named Mélanie huffed. "I'll be fine with that this time. But I hope the airline offers me some FRESH JUICE. It's the least they could do to apologize!"

"What an attitude!" Nicky commented.

Colette and Violet glanced behind them. Then Violet looked more closely at some paperwork in her lap.

"Hmmm," Violet said.

"What is it?" Nicky asked her friend. "Is something wrong?"

"Look," Violet said, pointing at the paper.

"That's the program for the International Archaeology Games, right?" Colette asked.

"That mouse in the photo —"

"Is on the FRENCH team!" Violet finished

Colette's sentence. "And she's sitting right behind us."

The three friends leaned over the program for a closer look.

"In addition to the French team, we're also competing against teams from Russia and Japan," Nicky commented.

"And there's a team from Italy, too," Colette added. "I hope they can tell us all the places we should visit!"

"I don't think we'll have much time for sightseeing, Coco," Violet warned her friend. "The schedule for the games seems really packed!"

"Did I hear that correctly?" came a voice behind them. The mouse named Mélanie popped up over their seats. "You're competing in the International Archaeology Games in Rome, too?"

"That's right," Paulina replied with a *smile*. Then she stuck out her paw.

"Hi, I'm Paulina," she said. "And these are my friends, the Thea Sisters. It's nice to meet you!"

Mélanie looked them **UP** and **DOWN** from the tips of their snouts to the ends of their tails.

"It's not worth getting to know you," she scoffed. "I can tell you'll be the first team eliminated from the competition."

And with that, she returned to looking out the WINDOW, ignoring everyone around her.

"I wouldn't listen to a thing she says," Colette told her friend. "It's going to be *marvemouse*, and I just know we'll do well in the COMPETITION!"

Teams Competing in the
International Archaeology Games

FROM TOKYO, JAPAN

Nami

Goro

Fumiko

Takeshi

Kuma

FROM MOSCOW, RUSSIA

Kirill

Irina

Roman

Nastia

Sergej

FROM PARIS, FRANCE

Aurélie

David

Mélanie

Jean-Marc

Carole

FROM MOUSEFORD ACADEMY

Violet

Paulina

Nicky

Pam

Colette

FROM ROME, ITALY

Mario

Flaminia

Alessandro

Rita

Luca

WELCOME TO ROME!

The plane finally landed at Fiumicino airport in Rome. The Thea Sisters and the students from the French team got their bags and headed for the exit.

"Look, there's someone waiting for us!" Nicky exclaimed, pointing to a young mouse. He was holding a large sign that read: Welcome, Teams for the International Archaeology Games!

"Great!" Colette said. "Let's go!"

"Come on," Pam said to the French team. "We can all go together!"

But Mélanie shook her head.

"*We* have personal transportation that my father has arranged, thank you," she replied snobbishly, her snout in the air.

At that moment a well-dressed rodent in a dark blue suit and sunglasses approached. After a short bow, he gestured for the French team to follow him to a silver limousine parked at the airport exit.

The Thea Sisters headed toward the young mouse with the SIGN.

"Hi!" Violet said, smiling. "We're the team from Mouseford Academy."

"*Welcome to Rome!*" the mouse replied. "I've heard a lot about your school. I would love to teach a class there one day . . ."

"Teach a class?" Colette repeated, confused.

"Yes!" he replied enthusiastically. "Oh, I'm sorry! I haven't introduced myself. I'm *Oreste*, Professor Amalia Angel's assistant."

Whoops!

He extended his paw toward Colette and in doing so dropped his sign.

Nicky bent down to pick it up.

"Thank you!" Oreste said as she passed it back to him. "Sorry, I'm a bit disorganized!"

"Don't worry," Nicky replied,

smiling. She noticed that Oreste was studying the crowd behind her, an **anxious** look on his snout. "If you're looking for the team from Paris, they already left. There was a private driver here waiting for them."

"**Really?!**" Oreste replied, a relieved look on his snout. "I thought I had **lost** them! Let's go, then! I didn't park far away."

Instead of a limousine, a **cozy** orange van with the local university's logo awaited them. The Thea Sisters climbed aboard happily, **excited** to begin their Roman adventure.

"Have you ever been to Rome before?" Oreste asked after they got on the road.

"No, this is our first visit!" the mouselets replied almost in unison.

"Well, you'll **love** it," Oreste said. "It's a **magical** place, especially if you like **archaeology!**"

The van entered the heart of the city, and the five mice pressed their snouts up against the windows. There was so much to take in here in the magnificent **Eternal City**!

"On your left across the Tiber River is Castel Sant'Angelo," Oreste explained.

"It was originally built as a mausoleum, but it later became a fortress."

"Wow," Colette squeaked.

Oreste turned **right** and drove down a series of alleys. Then he parked the van near an ancient-looking building.

"Here we are!" Oreste said. "This is the home of the **International Archaeology Games**. Go ahead and leave your bags in the VAN. We can grab them later."

The Thea Sisters followed Oreste into the building. He pointed them down a **LONG** corridor.

"The first door on the left is Professor Angel's office," he told them. "Unfortunately I have to **go** because I have class. I'll see you later!"

"Thanks for everything!" the mouselets called out as they waved good-bye. Then they scampered down the hallway and knocked on the office door.

Welcome!

A second later, a smiling Professor Angel appeared in the doorway.

"Welcome, mouselets!" she squeaked happily. "Please come in. I'm so glad you're here!"

The office was similar to the headmaster's office at Mouseford

Academy, though the walls were almost completely covered in frames.

The mouselets approached one of the walls, curious.

"We put up photos of all the previous winners of the **International Archaeology Games**," Professor Angel explained.

"Just imagine, mouselets," Violet said DReaMiLy. "Our picture could be up there, too!"

"We're so HONORED to have the opportunity to compete!" Nicky said. "You must be proud to involve so many students each year."

"It's true — I love the competition," Professor Angel replied. "But unfortunately this will be the last year. Our university doesn't have enough money to finance the games any longer."

"This is really the **LAST** one?" Pam asked in disbelief.

"Yes, but let's not focus on that," Professor Angel continued. "Let's talk about what awaits the **five** of you! The games are made up of various challenges held over two days.

"You will compete against **four** other teams. Tomorrow at nine we'll meet in the library, and Oreste and I will give you the instructions for the first challenge. Now, I imagine you want to go **UNPACK** your bags and rest for a bit. See you tomorrow!"

The Thea Sisters THANKED the professor and headed into the hallway. As they got farther from the professor's office, they heard a voice they recognized.

"If that driver had managed to find a **SHORTCUT**, we would have been here an hour ago!" the voice squeaked.

"Something tells me Mélanie had a problem with the traffic," Pam whispered to her friends as they *passed* the French team.

"I'm glad we got here quickly," Violet said, yawning. "I can't wait to unpack and maybe take a little **ratnap**!"

"Not me!" Colette said, bursting with energy. "You snooze, you lose, Violet. And you certainly don't become an archaeologist!"

Colette winked at her friend playfully, and the other mouselets all burst out laughing!

NEW FRIENDS

The Thea Sisters HEADED to the dorm in the building across the street. There, they met a guard named *Renzo* who showed them to their rooms on the first floor.

"Will all the teams be STAYING here?" Nicky asked him, curious.

"Yes, even the team from Rome will stay here during the event," Renzo told them. "They're also on the first floor. Here are the keys to your rooms."

He pointed to the two **DOORS** in front of them.

"If you have any problems, you can find me HERE!" he said helpfully.

"Thank you so much," Pam replied.

The room that Pamela and Colette chose

had a **bunk bed**, a small desk, and a closet. "But where's the bathroom?" Colette asked, worried.

"It's right here," Pam said as she opened a small door.

"Wow, it's so SMALL!" Colette gasped. "Where will I put all my makeup?"

Where will I put it all?

But Pam was distracted by a **delicious** smell wafting in from the hallway.

"Do you smell that?" she asked Colette.

"It smells like someone's COOKING," Colette replied.

A second later, Pam was out the door and hot on the **trail** of the appetizing aroma.

Colette quickly followed, and together the friends made their way to the kitchen. A group of mice were busy preparing a mountain of spaghetti with tomato sauce.

What a delicious smell!

"**HI!**" one of the mice greeted them kindly. "Who are you?"

"My name is Colette, and this is Pamela," Colette said. "We're from Mouseford Academy, and we're —"

"Famished!" Pam jumped in, finishing Colette's sentence.

The mouse burst out laughing.

"Do you want to join us?" he asked. "We're making a spaghetti dinner. I'm Alessandro, and this is Luca."

He gestured to the mouse standing next to him. Then he pointed to three others at the STOVE.

"And that's Rita, her sister Flaminia, and

Mario."

"Hi!" the other mice all said with friendly smiles and waves.

At that moment, the other Thea Sisters entered the room.

"We were wondering where you two had gone," Nicky said.

"I was taking a nap, but they DRAGGED me out of bed," Violet complained, yawning.

"Are these your classmates?" Luca asked.

"Yes," Colette replied. "That's Nicky, Paulina, and the half-asleep one is Violet."

"Very nice to meet you!" Luca replied. "We're all on the Italian team. Make yourselves at home!"

A moment later, everyone was seated around a large TABLE, sharing spaghetti and chatting.

"You're Professor Angel's students, right?" Nicky asked. "We took her seminar when she

visited Mouseford Academy."

"It was amazing!" Violet chimed in.

"Yes, she's the best!" Rita agreed enthusiastically.

"I'm so excited for the competition," Flaminia said. "What about you?"

"Yes, us too!" Violet replied. "Have you met the other teams yet?"

Alessandro nodded.

"The Japanese team is on the second floor along with the Russians," he said. "The French team is supposed to be staying on the third floor, but I heard they COMPLAINED about the dorm and they've gone to stay somewhere else."

"Was the mouse who complained tall with brown fur and green eyes?" Colette asked.

"I think so," Alessandro said. "Why? Do you know her?"

The Thea Sisters **EXCHANGED** a glance.

"We met her on the airplane," Nicky replied.

"Let's just say her complaints are nothing new!" Paulina added.

"Well, she made a big mistake leaving," Pam said while helping herself to some more pasta. "She missed out on all this DELICIOUS spaghetti!"

LET THE GAMES BEGIN!

The next morning, the Thea Sisters were the last to arrive in the library. Professor Angel and the four other teams were already there.

"And finally, the students from Mouseford

Academy are here," Professor Angel said with a smile. "They probably still have their ALARMS on Whale Island time!"

"Violet, if you hadn't taken forever to wake up, we would have been on time!" Nicky said under her breath.

Alessandro gave Violet a sympathetic look.

"I totally get it," he whispered. "My friends practically had to **DRAG** me out of bed this morning!"

I'm so sleepy!

I get it!

Violet smiled gratefully.

"Now that we're all here, let's go over the **RULES** of the games," the professor continued. "Oreste?"

Her assistant stepped forward.

"I will supply each team with all the materials you will need," Oreste said.

"There are two challenges," Professor Angel added. "The first will be held today, and the second one will be **tOMORROW**. You'll have to follow the clues, which will lead you through Rome.

Solve each puzzle as *quickly* as you can without using the Internet. For the first challenge, each team will split up: Two mice will stay in the library to provide research

support. The other team members will be out in the field."

One of the mice from the Russian team raised his paw.

"Won't the team from **Rome** have an advantage?" he asked. "After all, they already know the city!"

"You're RIGHT, Kirill," Professor Angel replied. "They may have a slight advantage during the first challenge. To make up for it, the Italian team will start fifteen minutes after the other teams during the second challenge. That should level the playing field."

Oreste handed each team a SEALED envelope.

"Here is the first thing you'll need for the COMPETITION," he told them.

Nicky opened the envelope.

"It's a map of Rome!" she observed.

Violet leaned over to get a closer *LOOK*.

"Yes," she agreed, "but it's a map of Rome from many centuries ago."

"That's right," Professor Angel piped up. "This map shows how Rome looked many, many years ago."

"But why would we need that?" Mélanie asked, her paws on her hips. "Rome looks totally different **TODAY**. This doesn't make any sense!"

"That's part of the challenge," the professor

replied, raising her eyebrow mysteriously. "You'll need to make a **trip to the past**, and this map will help."

"And now, let the games begin!" Oreste squeaked. He started his **stopwatch**.

The students looked at one another in confusion.

"But how?" asked one of the members of the Japanese team. "Where do we start?"

Alessandro smiled.

"I think that's part of the game," he said. "It's up to **us** to figure that out!"

Where do we start?

"That's right," Oreste agreed. "I suggest you split up and **GET TO WORK**!"

The Thea Sisters sat down and began EXAMINING the map. They searched for a clue that might serve as a starting point.

"There must be a way to figure out what the FIRST STEP is!" Colette exclaimed in frustration.

Meanwhile, Violet took advantage of their **LOCATION** in the library. She and Paulina grabbed some books about the development and planning of ancient Rome.

"Here, let's hope these help!" Violet exclaimed optimistically. She put two dusty books on the table in front of Pam.

"Ah . . . ah . . . achoo!" her friend sneezed noisily, knocking the map off the table.

"Oh, sorry!" Pam exclaimed. "It's all that **dust**!"

She picked up the paper, and something unusual caught her eye.

"Wait a minute!" Pam gasped. "There's something written on the back of this map!"

"It looks like a Riddle!" Colette exclaimed. "Well done, Pam!"

Nicky chuckled. "Just think — we had no idea what we were looking for, and all we had to do was turn over the map!"

Violet was already busy studying the message. She read it aloud:

"Julius Caesar's was the very first one,
And Trajan's was the last one done!"

Here we go . . .

Achoo!

"**Moldy mozzarella**, what does that mean?" Pamela asked, shaking her head.

"Julius Caesar and Trajan were two famous Roman emperors," Paulina replied thoughtfully. "Caesar lived in the first century AD, while Trajan reigned more than a century later. What could have been started by one and FINISHED by the other?"

"Paulina, do you have the notebook with our **archaeology** notes and research?" Violet asked.

"Yes, here it is!" her friend replied.

Julius Caesar

Traianus

"Can you find the pages on CAESAR?" Violet asked. "Maybe we noted some great works that he started, but that weren't finished until long after his **DEATH**!

I just know it has something to do with ancient Roman CONSTRUCTION . . ."

"Vi, you're a genius!" Colette said as Paulina bent her head over the *notebook* studiously. A few minutes later, Paulina looked up, a smile on her snout.

"I FOUND IT!"

THE FIRST STOP

Now that they had the answer to the riddle, the Thea Sisters were ready to officially begin the **International Archaeology Games**!

"Wait a minute!" Nicky said quickly. "Let's not forget what the professor said: Two of us have to **stay** here."

"You and I can stay, Nicky," Paulina proposed.

"Okay," Colette agreed. "Pam, Violet, and I will get moving!"

The three mice jumped up from the table, eager to begin. At that moment, three **Italian** mice on the other side of the room also stood up. Soon, the six mice were heading toward the exit TOGETHER.

"Professor!" Mélanie called out from across

the room. "THAT'S NOT FAIR!"

"What do you mean?" Professor Angel replied calmly.

Mélanie pointed to Colette, Pam, Violet, Alessandro, Luca, and Mario. The six mice paused at the door and looked back to see what was going on.

"Those six are leaving at the same time, but they're on **DIFFERENT TEAMS**!" Mélanie protested. "They shouldn't be working together!"

"That's true!" Kirill agreed, nodding his head. "Each group has to work INDEPENDENTLY."

The Thea Sisters were very surprised.

But the professor just shook her head.

They're working together!

"There are no rules against **collaborating**," she explained. "In fact, as long as there's no fighting or interfering, working together can be very **IMPORTANT**!"

Mélanie plunked back down in her seat, her arms crossed angrily. Then she turned to her teammates.

"*Hurry up* and find the answer!" she barked. "I'm not going to be the last to leave!"

"Go ahead, and GOOD LUCK!" the professor told the mice at the exit.

So Colette, Pam, and Violet left the building along with the three members of the Italian team.

"You figured out the first stop, right?" Colette asked them.

"It's the Imperial Fora!" Luca replied. "They were important public squares built during ancient times, and you can still visit today! Julius Caesar built the first one, and Trajan built the last!"

"Exactly!" Violet agreed, **smiling**.

"We have three scooters, and each one carries two passengers," Alessandro told them. "Would you like a ride?"

"Do you really mean that?" Pam asked in surprise. "That would **save us** a lot of time!"

"Then it's settled," Alessandro said decisively. "Come on, let's go!"

The Italians led the three mouselets toward three **SCOOTERS** that were parked at the side of the road. Each one of them had an extra **HELMET** under the seat. In a flash, the six mice were ready to go.

"Hold on tight, please," Alessandro told Violet as he stepped on the **GAS**.

A few moments later, they were weaving through the streets of Rome. Soon, they had reached the Imperial Fora.

"Thank you so much!" Pam exclaimed happily. "We never would have gotten here so QUICKLY without you guys!"

"A scooter is the best way to get around Rome," Alessandro said. "The traffic can be terrible!"

What a beautiful city!

"It may be quick, but it's not so great on the hairdo," Colette observed sadly as she removed her helmet.

Meanwhile, Violet was mesmerized by the Imperial Fora.

"Wow!" she exclaimed. "What a sight!"

"Alessandro asked. "It's impressive, isn't it?"

"What a beautiful city," Violet replied dreamily. "It must be AMAZING to pass places like this every day!"

"It is," he agreed. "It's true what they say, Rome is really an OPEN-AIR MUSEUM!"

"Come on," Mario interrupted them. "Let's not waste time chatting. Let's figure out what comes next!"

THE MYSTERIOUS RIDDLE

When the six mice got to the entrance to the Fora, Oreste was waiting for them. He handed each team a sealed envelope and wished them GOOD LUCK. Then all six mice entered the site together.

Good work, everyone!

Luca pulled out the MAP of ancient Rome and tried to orient himself.

"So, that **building** over there was built during Caesar's time," he said, pointing in one direction.

"And over there is the Forum of Augustus, while the largest one over there is Trajan's!"

Violet and Alessandro were holding each team's envelope.

"Should we open them **together**?" Alessandro asked.

"Yes!" Violet agreed.

Both envelopes contained the same question.

Violet read the clue aloud:

"Here's a new riddle for you to solve:

Around a bright center tireless wheels revolve.

Four wear rings, and four are bare.

Remove the last two — the answer is there!"

"What does this have to do with **archaeology**?" Mario wondered, confused.

"Maybe the riddle refers to people?" Luca suggested.

"Someone who is bright and wears rings might be a **QUEEN**," Colette mused.

"Why don't we all sit down and think this through **carefully**," Alessandro suggested.

So the six mice sat in a circle and began to toss out ideas.

"Maybe they're kings listed in chronological order," Pam suggested. "If you remove the last two, you would know which king . . ."

But Violet **SHOOK** her head.

"I don't know," she pondered. "I think the key is something else."

"Me too," Mario agreed. "What if the riddle isn't talking about historical figures but about something else. Maybe GEARS that turn?"

"And if they're TIRELESS, they're always spinning," Violet added. "But they must be turning around something . . ."

"It's so hot!" Colette complained as she fanned her snout with her hat. "The Roman SUN is really strong."

This sun is so hot!

"That's it!" Violet squeaked, LIGHTING UP. "Why didn't I think of it before! Well done, Coco!"

"The sun is the bright center!" Alessandro realized. "And the planets revolve around it."

"Of course!" Luca exclaimed. "Four of them have rings and four don't!"

"So the third from last planet is the answer," Pam said. "It's **SATURN**!"

Luca grinned. "I know exactly where to go!" he announced. "**FOLLOW ME!**"

A short while later, the six mice reached the remains of an ancient monument. Where there had once been an enormous facade, only a row of COLUMNS remained.

"These are the remains of the **Temple of Saturn**," Luca explained. "It was built in the fifth century AD and once contained a statue of Saturn."

"Great work, everyone!" Pam said. "But what do we do now?"

A NUMBERS PUZZLE

The six mice **stared** at the imposing Temple of Saturn. It was truly magnificent! But they still had no idea what to do next!

"WAIT A MINUTE!" Pam exclaimed suddenly. "The first riddle was on the back of the map. Did you check the other side of the letter Oreste gave us?"

Alessandro examined the paper and shook his head. "There's NOTHING written here, aside from the riddle," he said, disappointed.

But Violet was studying the Mouseford team's envelope closely. "I've got it!" she exclaimed, smiling brightly. "The rest of the CLUE is on the *inside* of the envelope."

She showed her friends a series of numbers written there. Underneath the numbers it said:

"The first challenge has come to an end. Figure out the answer, then return to your friends!"

"It's another riddle!" Pam said. "And this time there's `math`."

"No problem," Luca said. He **bent** over the envelope and studied it **closely**. "Let's see . . . there's probably a `logical sequence`. Maybe we should divide — no, multiply each group . . ."

18 5 13 1 19 20 / 15 14 15 20 20 18 16 20
5 / 17 12 1 13 20 / 9 13 5 13 4
9 / 3 13 18 20 12 15 19
20 12 / 17 18 19 9
19 20 9 19

After a few minutes of trying with N©
LUCK, Luca shook his head.

"Sorry, friends," he said with a shrug. "I
don't know how to SOLVE IT!"

"What if this is a message, not a math
problem?" Colette guessed. "Could it be a
kind of *code*?"

"If it's a code, Paulina's the expert," Pam

Paulina, we need your help!

said. "She'll be able to CRACK IT. Let's call her!"

"Great idea," Colette agreed.

A few moments later, Paulina and Nicky along with Flaminia and Rita from the Italian team, were all on squeakerphone from the library.

"What do you think, Paulina?" Violet asked.

"Could it be some kind of numeric code?"

"Maybe!" Paulina agreed. "First I would try the simplest key: Substitute each number with its corresponding letter of the alphabet. So, $a = 1$, $b = 2$, $c = 3$, and so on."

"Okay!" Mario replied. "But which alphabet should we use?"

"That's obvious," Flaminia replied. "The ancient Roman alphabet, of course!"

Rita scurried off to find a **LATIN** dictionary.

Rita read off the correct letters, and Violet scribbled some letters on a piece of paper.

"Here it is," she said, showing the translation to her friends:

Senatu popuusque rmanu inendi cnsumptum rstituit.

"It's very odd," Mario said, crinkling his forehead

in concentration. "It seems like it's a phrase in Latin, but there are some **MISTAKES.** *Popuusque, rmanu, inendi, rstituit* — it's meaningless when translated."

Alessandro shook his head.

"They aren't meaningless," he said. "They're just MISSING letters! Look!"

Alessandro pointed above their heads: The temple's **EIGHT COLUMNS** had a Latin inscription

on them that corresponded almost perfectly to the message.

"There are a few extra letters in the inscription," Alessandro said.

"I see what you mean," Colette agreed. "*S, L, O, S, C, O, O, E*. Those letters are on the columns, but not in our clue. But what does it mean?"

"*Sloscooe* is our clue?" Flaminia asked on the other end of the phone.

It's an anagram!

"Maybe the code is wrong," Rita added. "That word doesn't mean anything."

"But it does!" Paulina said suddenly. "It's only the most famous monument in **Rome**!

SLOSCOOE is an anagram* of COLOSSEO, the Italian word for 'Colosseum'!"

---

* An *anagram* is a word, phrase, or name formed by rearranging the letters of another word.

"Paulina, you're a GENIUS!" Colette squeaked. "You figured it out!"

"Now we need to get back to the university," Alessandro said. "It looks like both our teams have completed the first challenge!"

THE FIRST-ROUND RESULTS

A few hours later, all the teams were reunited in the university **LIBRARY**. The Thea Sisters and their new Italian friends were **anxious** to find out the day's results.

Finally, Professor Angel stood up and cleared her throat.

"Well done, everyone," she began. "You all **WORKED** hard and followed the rules — congratulations! And now let's get to the part I know you're all waiting for: today's results!"

Oreste stepped forward, a tablet in his **paws**.

He read from his **screen**: "For the first challenge of the Imperial Fora, first place goes to the team from **Moscow**!"

"Hooray!" the Russian team members squeaked happily, shaking one another's paws.

"The team from **Rome** is tied for second place with the team from **MOUSEFORD ACADEMY**!" Oreste continued.

The Thea Sisters and the Italians exchanged high fives.

"What?!" Mélanie huffed indignantly.

"In fourth place, we have the team from Paris," Oreste said. "And last but not least, the team from Tokyo is in fifth place."

"Try not to worry too much, Mélanie," her teammate Aurélie told her consolingly, putting her paw on Mélanie's arm. "It's just the first challenge. I'm sure we can **make it up**!"

But Mélanie brushed her off.

"Oh, come on," she scoffed. "This is no time for **excuses**. We were **PITIFUL**. First it took all that time to figure out that we needed to go to the Imperial Fora. Then David took forever to crack the **code** . . ."

David turned **redder** than a cheese rind.

"I-I'm sorry," he stammered, embarrassed. "I didn't think the ANSWER would be so easy . . ."

Mélanie didn't respond. Instead, she just stormed off and sat by herself in the corner, glaring at her teammates.

"Tomorrow will be a very busy day,"

Professor Angel reminded the students. "For now, though, you can all relax: Tonight we reserved a room at a **LOCAL RESTAURANT** so that you can rest and get to know each other better!"

I can't wait . . .

"**Fantastic!**" Pam squeaked happily. "Everyone knows it's easier to solve riddles and puzzles on a full stomach!"

The others burst out **laughing**.

Well, everyone but Mélanie, who was still sitting there, **pouting**.

"Come on, Mélanie, come to dinner with us," Kirill invited her. "We deserve to have some fun!"

But Mélanie just shook her head. "I don't usually **CELEBRATE** defeat," she replied. And without another squeak, she got up and strode out of the room.

Come with us!

No, thank you!

LUCIA'S RESTAURANT

Mélanie was the only participant in the games who didn't go to the dinner that evening. Everyone else met up at the dorm entrance, ready to walk to the restaurant together.

"Do you know this address?" Nicky asked Rita, showing her a piece of paper with the restaurant info Professor Angel had given her.

"I've heard of the street, but I don't know exactly where it is," Rita replied, shaking her head.

"Does anyone have a map that's more recent than one from the last MILLENNIUM?" Pam asked, laughing.

Takeshi took out a SMARTPHONE. "Why don't we use a more MODERN method?" he suggested.

The group FOLLOWED the directions on Takeshi's phone. They turned down narrow streets and crossed small squares. About twenty minutes later, they **found themselves** at the spot marked by the *glowing* dot. But the street was lined with unmarked buildings, and there was no sign of a restaurant *anywhere*!

"Are you sure you entered the right address, Takeshi?" Sergej asked in confusion.

"Yes, this is the **address**," he replied, blushing in embarassment. "But I agree that something seems off."

"It's hard to believe we're having more trouble finding a restaurant in

Let's use my GPS!

modern Rome than we did finding monuments that are **centuries old**!" Jean-Marc said with a **SMILE**.

Meanwhile, Paulina noticed a mouse in a checkered apron. She had just come around the corner carrying a few boxes.

"Excuse me, but do you know where we

might find a restaurant called **LUCIA'S**?" Paulina asked the mouse.

"You're already here!" she responded with a **chuckle**. "I am Lucia, and this is my trattoria!"

Only then did Paulina notice a sign partly covered in **ivy** hanging over a set of double doors. Inside, she could see tables and chairs.

"This is it!" Paulina squeaked excitedly. "Trattoria means 'restaurant'!"

"Thank goodmouse," Pam replied with a relieved sigh. "My stomach has been **grumbling** for at least half an hour!"

The group entered the picturesque restaurant and **SAT DOWN** around a large table covered with a cheerful red-and-white-checkered tablecloth. Lucia recommended a fried vegetable **appetizer**, several homemade **pasta** dishes, and a few typical *Italian meat* dishes.

They ordered a little bit of everything, curious to try as many *traditional* Roman dishes as possible. But after the first course, some of the students were already **full**!

"My stomach feels like it's going to burst!" Colette exclaimed. "I don't think I can eat another bite of the fried mozzarella or the grilled vegetables."

"Me either," Roman groaned. "I can't eat another bite!"

"Don't worry, I've got room for more!" Pam and Mario both exclaimed before they burst out *laughing*.

The dinner continued for hours, punctuated by laughter, friendly chatter, and lots of delicious food!

After **trying** a few cakes and desserts that Lucia had made herself, the group decided to **work off** their delicious meal with a stroll through the center of the city.

"I want to see the famous Spanish Steps," Aurélie said.

"Me too!" Kirill agreed.

"This time we don't need a map," Alessandro said with a smile. "I can take you there myself!"

The sun had set, and a *gentle* breeze was blowing.

"What a lovely night!" Colette remarked as she walked down a street lined with beautiful ancient buildings and charming shops.

"This road is called Via del Babuino," Luca explained. "And there is the Piazza di Spagna!"

"Look!" Violet exclaimed. "There are the Spanish Steps!"

"Can we **climb up**?" Carole asked, pointing to the large staircase that led to the famous obelisk at the top.

"Of course," Flaminia replied.

At the top of the stairs, some of the group began to take PICTURES while others sat down to enjoy the view.

"Are you enjoying the evening?" Alessandro asked Violet.

Violet nodded.

"This city is so incredible and unique," she said. "It's like nowhere I've ever been! My friends and I are LUCKY to be here."

I'm glad you like Rome!

"It's great to be able to show you around," Alessandro replied. Nearby, the group was gathering to take a photo. Everyone was smiling happily!

HERE WE GO AGAIN!

The next afternoon, the teams gathered in the main square in Rome's Monti neighborhood, just pawsteps away from the incredible Colosseum.

The teams stood around the octagonal fountain in the middle of the square. Everyone was eager to start the second day of the competition.

"For today's challenge, Oreste will give each team a package," Professor Angel announced. "You must wait to open it until your entire team arrives at the Colosseum. Each package contains a specific question.

"Oh, and one more thing: Today's competition will end at seven on the dot."

"But what if no one manages to solve the

puzzle by then?" Midori asked.

"In that case, we won't have a winner," Professor Angel replied with a smile. "But don't worry: That's never happened in previous competitions!"

I wonder what the challenge will be today!

"Are you ready, team?" Colette asked her friends.

The Thea Sisters smiled enthusiastically.

Oreste put up his paw to get everyone's attention.

"As we mentioned yesterday, the Italian team will have to start **fifteen minutes** after the other team since they are more familiar with the area."

Flaminia sighed. "Let's hope we can make up the time!" she told her teammates.

"Don't **WORRY**, we will!" Alessandro reassured her confidently.

"Good!" Professor Angel said. "Now, is everyone ready to begin?"

"Yes!" the students SQUEAKED enthusiastically.

"Ready, set . . . go!" Professor Angel cried.

Everyone except the Italian team scampered toward the Colosseum.

The Thea Sisters had to pause for a moment to admire what they saw at the end of the road. They glimpsed an **incredible** view of the ancient Roman amphitheater they had seen so many times in their **art** and HISTORY textbooks.

"It's even more beautiful than I imagined," Violet remarked.

"It is incredible," Nicky agreed. "But look — the other teams are WAY ahead of us!"

She pointed toward the French, Russian, and Japanese teams, who had almost reached the Colosseum already.

"You're right!" Pamela exclaimed. "Let's go!"

And she *DARTED OFF* at top speed after the other contestants.

It took a few minutes to reach the Colosseum and a few more for them to get inside.

"Now we can open the **package**," Paulina said eagerly as she began to unwrap it.

CALCULATIONS AT THE COLOSSEUM

"There's a DRAWING in here!" Paulina exclaimed.

The Thea Sisters gathered around her to examine the contents of the package.

"Holey cheese, what do you think it is?" Pam asked. "It looks like a GEOMETRY problem!"

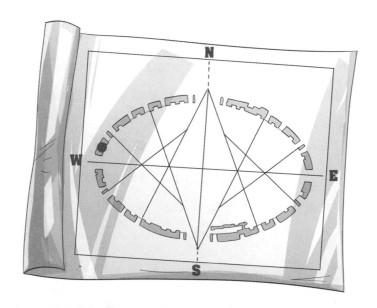

Violet analyzed the drawing for a few minutes.

"I think I understand, mouselets," she said at last. "Judging from the shape, this looks like a FLOOR PLAN of the Colosseum!"

"Genius, Vi!" Colette told her friend. "Why didn't we *REALIZE* that right away?"

"I think we need to head toward this marking," Nicky said, pointing to a red dot on the perimeter of the building in the drawing.

"But which side is that?" Colette asked.

"We **entered** from the south entrance," Violet observed. "So we need to go west."

"Let's hurry!" Nicky said, and a second later, she was off.

Her friends **FOLLOWED**, moving around the perimeter of the building until they reached the spot that corresponded to the red dot on the map.

"Let's look carefully," Paulina urged them. "The next clue must be around this archway!"

Paulina, Pam, Nicky, and Colette began to **explore** every inch of the structure around them. But Violet stood quietly off to the side, lost in thought.

"Vi, aren't you going to help us?"

Let's check the archway!

There must be a clue!

Hmm . . .

Colette asked.

"Yes, of course," Violet said distractedly. "I was just thinking that this seems too easy . . ."

"What do you mean?" Colette asked.

"I just think we might be MISSING something," Violet replied.

"There's nothing here!" Nicky exclaimed.

"I haven't found anything, either," Pam said.

"Maybe we're in the wrong spot," Paulina added.

"Or maybe Violet is right and we missed something," Colette reflected. "Paulina, did you look all over the package?"

"Yes, I thought so," Paulina replied. "Wait there's something else here!"

She pulled out a *sheet of paper*.

"Sorry, mouselets," Paulina apologized. "I was in such a rush, I didn't see it!"

"It's okay," Nicky reassured her friend.

"Let's take a look!"

"More **MATH**," Pam groaned.

"Don't worry, this is an 𝔼𝔸𝕊𝕐 one," Paulina assured her. "Each picture corresponds to a number.

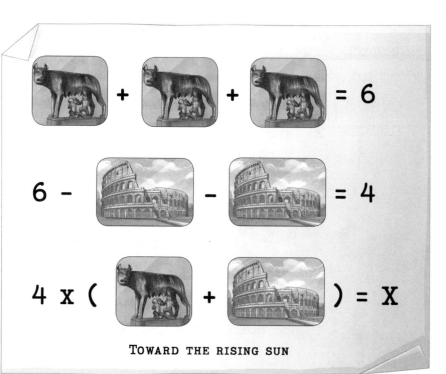

TOWARD THE RISING SUN

For example, if 6 equals 3 Capitoline Wolves, we need to figure out what number repeated three times equals 6."

"The answer is 2!" Colette called out.

"Yes," Paulina agreed. "And if 6 minus 2 Colosseums makes 4, that means the Colosseum equals 1. Finally, the Capitoline Wolf plus the Colosseum makes three, and 4 times 3 equals 12."

"But what does that tell us?" Nicky asked. "I think it has something to do with this line at the bottom of the PAGE: *Toward the rising sun,*" Violet said. "What if we count 12 arches east of the red dot, in the direction of the rising sun?"

Without wasting another minute,

the five mouselets walked to the right, counting the archways.

"Still nothing?" a familiar voice squeaked suddenly.

The Thea Sisters stopped in their pawtracks. Mélanie had strayed from her group. "You won't beat us this time," she said. "We've almost figured out the next clue!"

"Good for you, Mélanie," Paulina remarked. "Now if you'll excuse us, we still need to FINISH this riddle. We're almost there!"

Mélanie wrinkled her nose.

"What do you mean?" she asked skeptically. "You were fumbling around in the dark until two minutes ago, and now you've almost solved the puzzle?"

"Why don't you worry about your team instead of ours?" Colette asked, a little IRRITATED.

Mélanie just shrugged. "I do what I want," she said. "And if you think I care at all about anyone else, you're fooling yourselves!"

Then she turned around and marched off.

"She's so mean!" Colette huffed.

"Forget about it, Coco," Nicky said. "She isn't worth the time. And here's the twelfth arch!"

"LOOK!" Paulina exclaimed. "There's something in that corner!"

She leaned down and picked up a BOX that had *Mouseford* written on it.

"Hooray! We found the clue!" the mouselets squeaked happily.

Meanwhile, Violet noticed that instead of returning to her team, Mélanie had ducked behind another column to make a *phone call* . . .

WE NEED SOME HELP

Inside the box the Thea Sisters found a piece of paper that read "**LAST CLUE**" and a small wooden tile.

"There's something written on it!" Pam squeaked.

Paulina studied the tile closely.

"It says, *The first complete treatise of* medicine *in Latin, page thirty*," she read. Then she turned the tile over. "There's just one word on the back."

The mouselets looked at one another.

"Does anyone have any **idea** what the

treatise of medicine could be?" Colette asked.

The five friends shook their heads in **silence**.

"And Bassianus?" Pam asked. "It means nothing to me. Could it be a place?"

"I don't know," Violet admitted, a bit disheartened.

Nicky shook her head, too.

"If only we could use the **Internet**," Pam said with a sigh. "We could find out the answers so quickly!"

"The professor's rules were clear," Paulina said firmly. "We have to figure it out on our own."

"Let's not lose hope, mouselets," Colette said. "We'll **FIND** a solution this time, too. I'm sure of it!"

"You're right, Coco, but we could use some help," Violet pointed out.

"Let's think carefully," Paulina said. "Before the Internet, where did mice go for answers?"

"Of course!" Nicky squeaked. "They went to the **LIBRARY**. Let's go!"

Once they were outside the Colosseum, though, the friends **STOPPED**.

"But how will we find a library?" Pam asked.

"We could go back to the university," Nicky

suggested. "But that would take a lot of time."

"I have an idea," Colette said. Then she approached an elderly mouse who was crossing the square. A few minutes later, Colette returned to the group, smiling *brightly*.

"I have great news!" she announced. "There's a library less than a ten-minute walk from here! That mouse was really helpful: She even gave me directions. Follow me!"

The Thea Sisters followed Colette down a road that crossed through **archaeological** sites that had once been ancient Roman squares.

"**LOOK!**" Violet pointed out. "On our left is the Trajan Forum. And there's the famous Trajan's Column over there!"

The FIVE FRIENDS approached to admire the column, which was covered in carvings and topped with an ornate statue.

"Remember when Professor Angel talked about this column in her seminar at Mouseford Academy?" Paulina asked. "I never **imagined** I would have the chance to see it in the fur!"

"Violet, didn't the professor tell us the bas-relief shows the **BATTLE** between the Romans and the Dacians for control of the ancient region of Dacia near the **DANUBE RIVER**?" Colette asked.

But Violet didn't seem to hear her. Instead, she seemed to be focusing on something behind Colette.

"Vi?" Colette repeated, a little **louder.**

"Huh?" Violet replied. "Oh, Dacia . . . yes, of course. That's right."

"Is everything **OKAY**?" Colette asked her friend. "You seem distracted."

Violet lowered her squeak to a whisper.

"Sorry," she told her friends. "I just feel like someone is **following** us. Have you noticed **ANYTHING**?"

The others shook their heads.

"Maybe the stress of the competition is bothering you," Nicky replied. "But we're almost at the end!"

"Yes, you're probably right," Violet agreed. "I **am** feeling anxious about the competition."

CLUE!

VIOLET THINKS SOMEONE MAY BE FOLLOWING THEIR TEAM. DID YOU NOTICE ANYTHING — OR ANYONE — SUSPICIOUS ON PAGE 102?

"Come on, team!" Nicky said encouragingly. "The library is super close, and our next task isn't going to be easy. We need to find the first complete treatise of medicine in Latin and see if we can figure out what the mysterious word BASSIANUS means."

The five mice scampered quickly toward the library.

feel like we're being followed . . .

TOGETHER AGAIN

Once they were inside the library, the team SPLIT UP the work: Pam, Nicky, and Violet took the task of figuring out what the first MEDICAL treatise in Latin was, while Colette and Paulina tried to figure out the meaning of the word *Bassianus*.

"I think we should head for the archives," Paulina suggested. "It contains a list of all the books in the library!"

"Good idea, Paulina," Colette agreed. "Even without the Internet, the library's COMPUTERS might be really useful!"

Meanwhile, the other three mice headed for the MEDICAL books.

"These are the first treatises, but they're in ancient Greek," Nicky pointed out.

"Let's look over here," Pam suggested as she moved farther down the row of books. "I think that **SHELF** has books that are in Latin."

Violet began to leaf through some ancient volumes. After a few minutes, she squeaked in excitement.

"I might have found it!" she cried. "This book cites the treatise *De Medicina*, by Aulo Cornelio Celso."

Let's see . . .

"It's not here on the shelf," Nicky said after she had looked. "Let's check the **computer** archive."

"Hi!" a familiar voice squeaked suddenly.

"Luca! Mario!" Nicky exclaimed in *surprise*. "What are you doing here?"

Let's try this one . . .

"We're trying to decipher our **CLUE**," Luca explained. "But we're running behind since we started fifteen minutes after everyone else."

"Where's Alessandro?" Violet asked.

"He's still at the entrance," Mario replied. "The **guard** is a former classmate of his, so he stopped to say hello."

At that moment, Colette and Paulina reappeared.

"We figured out what BASSIANUS means!" Colette burst out excitedly.

Then she saw the members of the Italian team. "Hi! You're here, too?"

"They're doing research, just like us," Nicky explained. "Though they're a bit further behind because of their late start."

"Why don't we join forces again?" Colette proposed. "Even if we have different clues, the answer is the same for everyone.

We don't want to take advantage . . .

And we're already in a good place!"

The Italian team exchanged a glance, looking unsure.

"We don't want to take advantage of your KINDNESS," Flaminia said at last. "And I'm not sure if we're allowed to collaborate at this point."

"Don't you **remember** what Professor Angel said?" Violet reminded them. "As long as everyone is on the same page, working together can be **VERY USEFUL!**"

"That's true!" Rita agreed. "Why not? What have you figured out so far?"

"We have two clues: the word BASSIANUS and a specific page of the first treatise of medicine in Latin," Nicky said, filling in the Italian team.

"And we just discovered that *Bassianus* is a name," Colette said. "It was **Emperor Caracalla**'s name at birth!"

Caracalla

"And we've figured out that the treatise we need to find is called **De Medicina**," Violet explained. "It's in this library, but we don't know exactly where."

"Then let's go back to the **ARCHIVE**!" Paulina suggested.

UNDERGROUND RESEARCH

As the group of students headed down the **hallway** toward the archives, they crossed paths with Alessandro.

"You're all here?" he asked, **stunned**.

"The Mouseford team proposed that we **team up** again," Luca explained. "They almost solved the riddle!"

"We only have ten minutes before the **library** closes," Rita observed, looking at her watch. "We need to hurry!"

"I wouldn't worry too much about that," Alessandro said, smiling. "The library guard, Giovanni, was my classmate. I explained why we're here, and he said we can stay as long as we need to!"

"Excellent!" everyone cheered.

"Now let's go look for the book that will help us solve the Riddle: *De Medicina* by Paulo Cornelio Gelso!" Pam said.

Violet chuckled.

"What an imagination you have, Pam," Violet said. "His name is Aulo Cornelio Celso!"

"Did I say something different?" Pam asked, confused. "Oh well. You know who I mean!"

The group split up, and each took a different corner of the library.

Violet and Alessandro PAIRED UP.

"Who was this Aulo Cornelio Celso?" Alessandro asked.

"He was a **ROMAN** who

Excellent! We can keep working!

wrote about medicine in the ancient Roman world," Violet explained. "In *De Medicina*, he united all the Greek and Latin knowledge into one book!"

"I'm afraid there's no sign of it here," said a disappointed Alessandro, shaking his head.

Violet glanced around at her friends, who were also searching for the book. "The others haven't found it, either," she said, **disappointed**.

"What if we look downstairs?" Alessandro suggested.

"What do you mean?" Violet asked.

AULO CORNELIO CELSO

An encyclopedist who lived in Rome in the first half of the first century AD. Even though he wasn't a medical professional, he wrote what was considered the first complete treatise of medicine in Latin. *De Medicina* is divided into eight books dedicated to nutrition, medicines, and surgery.

"It might be in the basement archive," Alessandro explained. "The librarian might have moved it down there at some point."

"But that would be **LOCKED**, wouldn't it?" Violet asked.

"Yes, but I have the keys," Alessandro replied with a wink. "Giovanni gave them to me."

"Okay, let's try it!" Violet agreed enthusiastically.

The pair quickly headed toward a metal door.

On the other side of the door, a long, winding staircase led down to the basement.

Alessandro flicked a switch, and a dim light illuminated the steps. "Let's go!" Violet whispered.

I have the keys!

This way!

At the end of the stairs was another *door*. Alessandro opened it with the key, which jammed in the lock.

"Let's not waste any time," he said. "I'll grab the key on our way out!"

On the other side of the door, a small hallway LED to a dusty room full of old volumes.

"Achoo!" Alessandro sneezed. "Excuse me. It's just so dusty!"

"Here it is!" Violet exclaimed happily

as she pulled a book off the shelf. "Look!"

Alessandro took the book that she handed him. Etched in golden letters on the spine were the words *De Medicina*.

"WOW, this is really it!" Alessandro exclaimed. "Now what do we do?"

"We need to look at page . . . at page . . . oh, I can't remember!" Violet replied in dismay.

"Don't worry," Alessandro reassured her.

"We can go upstairs and show the others. Someone will remember the PAGE NUMBER."

Violet followed Alessandro back toward the stairs. At the end of the hallway, though, a TERRIBLE surprise awaited them.

"The door is stuck!" Alessandro exclaimed. He pushed hard, but it wouldn't budge. "It feels like it's locked!"

"But how?" Violet asked. "I left the door OPEN, right?"

"I don't know," Alessandro admitted. "And the keys are on the other side. What could have HAPPENED?"

"Maybe a gust of wind blew it closed," Violet guessed.

"This stinks worse than MOLDY CHEESE!" Alessandro said, sighing. "We really didn't need this setback."

"We're down here!" Violet yelled loudly as she pounded on the door. "OPEN UP!"

"I don't think they can hear you," Alessandro said. "Should we try to call them? Do you have your **phone**?"

Violet pulled out her phone.

"Oh no," she said in defeat. "There's no service down here."

"Then I don't think there is anything we can do," Alessandro said, **disheartened**. "We just have to wait."

WHO COULD IT BE?

Meanwhile, the others were still busy looking for the **BOOK** upstairs.

"Hey, Coco! Did you find anything?" Nicky asked, approaching her friend.

Colette sighed. "No, not yet, unfortunately. **YOU**?"

Nicky shook her head. "Me neither."

Can you give me a paw, please?

"Nicky, can you give me a hand?" Flaminia asked as she struggled to lift a **HUGE BOX** that was blocking the lower part of the shelf.

"Of course!" Nicky replied.

"Where could it be?" Colette mumbled. "We've

looked everywhere . . ."

Then she noticed an **old** cabinet in the hallway, and she tried to **SEE** what was inside it. But instead, the glass door of the cabinet reflected something *outside* it — the silhouette of someone *rushing* quickly out of the library.

"Who's that leaving?" she wondered aloud, confused. "We haven't solved the last *riddle* yet!"

She stuck her head into the hallway to get a better look, and she realized it wasn't one of her **friends** or someone from the Italian team. Instead, it was a strange mouse dressed in blue.

"Hey!" Colette called after him, but the mouse didn't stop.

"Colette!" Luca called to her.

"Did you notice that stranger leaving the `library` just now?" Colette asked him. "I thought we were the only ones here . . ."

"I didn't see anyone," Luca replied hurriedly. "Have you seen Alessandro and Violet by any chance? We can't find them **anywhere**!"

"No," Colette replied in surprise. "I've been in this room the whole time, and I haven't **seen** them in ages."

Who could it be?

"We can't FIGURE OUT where they ended up," Luca said, sounding worried.

"It's not like Violet to disappear in the middle of a project," Colette said. "Maybe they left to look for more CLUES somewhere else? Did you try calling them?"

"Alessandro left his phone on the table over

CLUE!

A MYSTERIOUS FIGURE LEFT THE LIBRARY IN A HURRY... WHO WAS IT? AND WHAT WERE THEY DOING IN THE LIBRARY AFTER IT WAS CLOSED?

there," Luca replied. "And we tried calling Violet, but there was *no answer.*"

"**How strange**," Colette said. "But if Alessandro left his phone here, surely they haven't gone far."

"That's true," Luca agreed. "The others are **LOOKING** in the courtyard. Will you help me look in the other rooms?"

"Of course!" Colette exclaimed. "There's no time to lose!"

A SECRET PASSAGE

Meanwhile in the **BASEMENT**, Alessandro and Violet tried to come up with a plan. Alessandro pulled on the door one more time.

"It's useless!" he squeaked. "The door won't budge."

"What bad luck!" Violet said. "Just **WHEN** we had found the book, we get stuck down here with no way to reach our friends. There has to be another **way out**, don't you think?"

Violet and Alessandro began to search the basement carefully, looking for a second exit.

After a thorough search, though, they found themselves right back where they had started!

"There's no other door," Alessandro said, disappointed.

"I know," Violet added with a sigh. "There

isn't even a WINDOW down here!"

Feeling disheartened, Violet sat down in a corner against the **WALL**. Suddenly, she felt a chilly draft at her back. Surprised, she turned to see where the cool air was coming from. There seemed to be a crack in the smooth **STONE** wall.

"Alessandro!" she said. "Can you come over here?"

Huh?

"Sure," he replied quickly. "Did you **FIND** something?"

"Do you feel that *breeze*?" Violet asked. "It seems to be coming from the **WALL**!"

Alessandro took a step closer. "Yes, I feel it!" he said, surprised. "There must be an opening back here . . ."

He **KNOCKED** on the wall.

"It seems thinner right here," he observed.

Violet knocked as well.

"It sounds hollow," she agreed.

The two friends began to push the huge slab of **STONE** until it started to move.

"Maybe we **FOUND** a secret passage!" Alessandro said.

With one last push, the stone wall opened up to reveal a staircase carved in stone.

"**LOOK!**" Violet exclaimed.

"Yes!" Alessandro squeaked happily. "We're free!"

And with that, he scampered up the steps.

Violet followed closely behind. As the two mice climbed, the light got **BRIGHTER** and **BRIGHTER**. Finally, they reached a grate. Alessandro pushed it with his paw, moving it aside.

"This is the library courtyard!" Violet exclaimed, stunned. She **popped** out of the passage right behind her friend.

"Vi, Alessandro!" Paulina exclaimed, running toward them. "What were you doing down there?"

"We looked for you two everywhere!" Mario said. "We were **worried**!"

Everyone gathered in the courtyard, where

the Thea Sisters gave Violet a big **hug**.

"It's a long story, but we can tell you about it later," Alessandro said. "The important thing is that we found the book we were looking for!"

Violet held it out to show everyone. "Now we can solve the RIDDLE!" she squeaked happily.

"Amazing!" Nicky cried. "Let's go back inside."

"Yes, and let's *HURRY*," Mario added. "Time is about to *run out*!"

WE'RE ALMOST THERE!

Once they were back inside the library, Alessandro returned to the basement archive to retrieve the keys. But to his great surprise, the door was closed and the keys were GONE!

"They're gone?" Violet asked when he told her. "But how? Maybe they FELL somewhere when the door slammed closed?"

"I have no idea," Alessandro replied with a shrug. "Let's look for the keys LATER; we can't waste any more time. Meanwhile I'll ask Giovanni to stop by and lock up the library. But right now we need to focus on FIGURING OUT the puzzle in this book!"

Violet placed the **ancient** volume they had

found in the basement on the table in front of everyone. "Do you remember what page we were supposed to look at in the clue?" she asked her friends.

"Yes, PAGE THIRTY," Paulina replied confidently.

Violet carefully turned to page thirty and began to read in silence. Everyone held their **breath**.

"This section is about medical cures, and the passage on this page talks about water treatments," Violet said at last.

"Hmm, water," Colette said. "Maybe the last spot is the Tiber River?"

"Or maybe it's a pool!" Pam exclaimed.

"I don't think so," Rita said slowly.

"Did you solve the riddle, then?" Flaminia asked her teammate.

Rita nodded.

"I think we need to go to the baths!" she said

"**BATHS?!**" Colette repeated.

"Of course!" Nicky exclaimed. "The Baths of Caracalla! The two clues only make sense if you put them *together*: Emperor Caracalla and a water cure means the answer is the baths that he built, right?"

THE BATHS OF CARACALLA

The baths were opened by Emperor Caracalla in AD 216 and have largely been preserved today. In ancient Rome, the public bath was an important meeting place for people, who gathered there to bathe, play sports, and socialize. Inside there was a cold bath (the frigidarium), a hot bath (the calidarium), and a mid-temperature bath (the tepidarium). There was also the natatio, a large open-air swimming pool.

The baths of Caracalla had a rectangular layout. The majestic circular calidarium had large windows, while the frigidarium and the natatio were farther inward. The baths were expanded by the emperors who followed Caracalla, but they were abandoned in the sixth century. Ten centuries later, they were rediscovered and preserved as archaeological treasures!

Rita nodded, a **smile** on her snout.

"Where are these baths?" Nicky asked.

"About a fifteen-minute ᴡalк from here," came Mario's reply.

Paulina looked at her watch.

"It's six forty-seven right now," she said. "We **ONLY** have thirteen minutes!"

"If we leave right now, we can make it," Nicky said with determination. "*Let's go!*"

We only have a few minutes!

We can do it!

Let's go!

"Who knows the way?" Pam asked.

"I do!" Mario squeaked. "**FOLLOW ME!**"

A moment later, the group was scampering at full speed toward the last stop of the games: the Baths of Caracalla!

BY A WHISKER!

"Fifty-seven . . . fifty-eight . . . fifty-nine . . . It's seven o'clock!" Professor Angel announced. "I **OFFICIALLY** declare this the end of the **International Archaeology Games**."

The games are over!

She handed the **stopwatch** back to Oreste.

"And the **winner** of this year's competition is —"

"**Here we are!**" cried the Thea Sisters and the Italian team as they sprinted from the main road into the Baths of Caracalla.

"**DID WE MAKE IT ON TIME?**" Colette asked, breathless.

The professor shook her head.

"I'm very sorry, but *TIME IS UP*. You missed it by a whisker!"

"We won, and you didn't even finish the challenge in time!" Mélanie commented with an air of SATISFACTION. "You should have dropped out while you had the chance."

"Listen here . . ." Rita began, irritated. But Flaminia put out a paw to stop her sister.

"Let it go, Rita," she said. "We lost."

"Unfortunately, the competition is over," Oreste confirmed. "The **first team** to arrive was the French team, followed by the team from Moscow, and then the team from Tokyo. I'm very sorry, but the teams from Rome and from Mouseford Academy did not qualify because they arrived after the deadline."

"What a shame," Colette said. "And we tried so hard to make it!"

Violet sighed. "If we hadn't been locked

in the basement at the library, we probably would have made it."

"*Excuses, excuses*," Mélanie taunted.

But Professor Angel cut her off. "The awards

You lost!

Wait . . .

But . . .

ceremony will take place at the UNIVERSITY," she told the teams. "I'll meet you all there in the Great Hall in exactly one hour."

A STRANGE
COINCIDENCE . . .

The Thea Sisters and the Italian students were upset and disappointed.

"This stinks worse than moldy cheese," Luca said, sighing. "We were only a few seconds too late!"

"It's really **unfair**," Alessandro complained. "It's not our fault we were locked in the basement."

"Sometimes one small SETBACK is enough to keep you from reaching your goals," Paulina said.

"But at least we know we did our **best**," Violet reminded her friends.

"And it was an incredible experience!" Colette said, smiling.

The group of students was heading toward a bus that would take them back to the UNIVERSITY when Colette noticed something strange out of the corner of her eye. Her smile faded.

"What's wrong, Coco?" Nicky asked, noticing her friend's EXPRESSION.

"So that's who that mouse was!" Colette exclaimed. She POINTED to a rodent dressed in blue and talking to Mélanie nearby.

"What do you mean, Coco?" Pam asked, confused.

"That's Mélanie's driver!" Colette squeaked. "And I'm almost positive he was the rodent I saw leave the library in a *hurry* while we were looking for Vi and Alessandro."

"**Holey cheese!**" Pam exclaimed. "That's a **strange coincidence!**"

"It seems too strange for it to be a **coincidence**," Violet said thoughtfully.

CLUE!

THE THEA SISTERS SAW MÉLANIE'S DRIVER WHEN THEY ARRIVED AT THE AIRPORT. GO BACK AND CHECK TO SEE IF IT'S THE SAME MOUSE! WHAT WOULD MÉLANIE'S DRIVER BE DOING IN THE LIBRARY?

By now the members of the other teams had left the baths. Violet watched the mouse dressed in blue as he exited in the opposite direction. As he walked, a small **shiny** object fell to the ground.

Violet quickly dashed over to pick it up.

"Look!" she said, holding it up for her friends to see. "He dropped this."

It was a small key chain in the shape of an anchor with **TWO KEYS** attached.

"Wait a minute, those are the keys to the library!" Alessandro said, stunned.

"Then I was right!" Colette exclaimed. "That *was* the mouse I saw leaving the library."

"I don't **understand**," Luca said. "Why would Mélanie's driver be in the library with us? And what is he doing with those **KEYS**?"

"Are we really sure these are the keys to the library?" Mario asked, **doubtful**. "Maybe he just has the same key chain."

"Let's **check**," Alessandro suggested. "I'll call my friend Giovanni, the library guard!"

A moment later, Alessandro hung up the phone.

Hi, Giovanni!

"Good news, mouselets," he said, **smiling**. "Giovanni lives nearby and can be here in a few minutes."

As soon as Giovanni arrived, he pulled out a set of keys.

"This is my **SPARE SET**," he explained. "They're identical to these, so they must be the ones I loaned you, Alessandro."

"Now it all **makes sense!**" Violet said, her eyes **LIGHTING UP**.

"It does?" Paulina asked. "But how?"

"Remember when we were heading TOWARD the library and I had the feeling someone was following us?" Violet explained.

The Thea Sisters nodded.

"I think it was Mélanie's driver," Violet continued. "He must have been keeping an EYE on us."

"What?" Pam gasped in surprise. "But why?"

"Think about it," Violet said. "Mélanie wanted to win at all costs, and her team was behind. She could have asked her driver to follow us and slow us down."

"OF COURSE!" Alessandro chimed in. "Colette saw that rodent in the library. He must have watched Violet and me go down to the basement. Then he closed the door behind us, locked it, and took the key!"

"And that's when I saw him *DART* off!" Colette added.

"If that's really the way things went, we need to tell Professor Angel before the awards ceremony," Flaminia said. "Mélanie's team *CHEATED*!"

EVERYONE STOP!

The Thea Sisters and Italian students didn't have time to wait for the bus. They decided to *sprint* all the way back to the university!

"All this running is really making me HUNGRY!" Pam complained as she hustled along with the others.

"Hang on, Pam," Nicky said encouragingly.

"Tonight we'll make time for a huge Italian dinner. But for now, we need to RUUUUNNNN!"

"We made it!" Luca cried as the group arrived in front of the university building.

Alessandro led the group through the FRONT DOOR and toward the Great Hall. When they entered the room, all the other teams were already there, along with other students and instructors from the university.

Professor Angel was standing on a platform at the center of the room, ready to **present** the winner's cup to the French team.

"**STOP!**" Alessandro yelled.

"What's this about?" Professor Angel asked. "Why are you **interrupting** the ceremony, Alessandro?!"

"You haven't given up yet?!" Mélanie huffed, crossing her arms. "My team won, and you can't take away my **PRIZE**!"

"We don't care about that," Violet explained quickly. "But we want to shed **LIGHT** on what really happened during the last leg of the competition. Professor, we would like to speak

with you. It's very important!"

The professor hesitated for a moment, but when she saw the serious looks on their snouts, she agreed.

"Okay," she told them. "What is it?"

Violet BRIEFLY explained what happened in the library.

"We believe Mélanie intentionally **trapped** us to slow us down," she concluded.

"And that mouse over there helped!" Mario said.

He pointed to Mélanie's driver, who was standing off to the side.

"Oh, come on," the rodent grumbled. "At most I made you lose a little time!"

"What a fool," Mélanie growled

ANGRILY, glaring at the mouse in the blue suit.

Professor Angel was aghast.

"So all of this is true, Mélanie?" she asked quietly. "You sabotaged the other teams so your team would win?"

"I . . . N-no . . . W-well . . ." Mélanie stammered.

"She's squeakless for once!" Colette whispered, chuckling.

Professor Angel gave Mélanie a severe look.

"This is a **serious** violation of the rules, and it goes against the spirit of the games," she said. "Furthermore, this kind of behavior could have had dangerous consequences! The Paris team is **DISQUALIFIED** from the competition."

"Oh no!" Mélanie's teammates groaned in dismay.

"That means we won!" Roman exclaimed.

"Yes, the rankings have changed," Professor Angel said, nodding. "The winner of this year's **International Archaeology Games** is the team from Russia."

Kirill, Irina, Roman, Nastia, and Sergej rejoiced, shaking paws before they **ACCEPTED** the golden cup.

"In second place, we have the team from Tokyo," Professor Angel continued, handing the silver cup to Takeshi, who thanked her with a series of bows. "Congratulations! This year, we **do not have** a third-place winner because the French team was **DISQUALIFIED** for foul play, and the Italian team and the team from Mouseford Academy didn't finish in time."

Mélanie sighed. "Well, it just didn't work out for us this year," she told her teammates. "I did **EVERYTHING** I could to help, but I guess it wasn't enough."

The French team looked angrier than a herd of hungry cats.

"We trusted you and worked our hardest, and you **spoiled it** for all of us," Aurélie squeaked.

"I can't believe you cheated, and **BEHIND**

OUR BACKS, too!" David continued. "You're not welcome in our study group anymore."

"You're on your own, Mélanie," Carole said sadly. Then she and her teammates walked away.

"What a **THANKLESS** bunch!" Mélanie grumbled. "After everything I've done for this team!"

But no one was paying attention to her. Instead, the Russian team and the Japanese team were busy celebrating their wins.

ONE MORE THING . . .

After the awards ceremony, **PROFESSOR ANGEL** called the Thea Sisters into her office.

"You all did a great job in the competition," she said. "You really gave it your all. I'm sorry your team was disqualified because of the time limit, but I want you to know how much I appreciate your effort and your **TEAM SPIRIT**."

"Thank you, Professor!" Colette replied. "Participating in the games was a terrific experience and a real honor."

"I'll be sure to write to your headmaster to let him know how **impressed** I was with his students!" Professor Angel said, smiling.

"Thanks so much!" Nicky replied, shaking the professor's paw.

One by one, the Thea Sisters said good-bye to Professor Angel and Oreste. Violet was the last to go, and she was unusually quiet.

"Is everything okay, Violet?" Oreste asked.

"I noticed something strange, but I really don't want to waste your time . . ."

"What's this about?" asked Professor Angel, CURIOUS.

"Well, when Alessandro and I managed to get out of the library's basement archives, we ended up in a SECRET PASSAGE that led to the courtyard," Violet explained.

"Go on," Oreste urged her, intrigued.

"I noticed a recess in the wall as we scampered through the passageway," Violet said. "And now that I think about it, I think there was something in there."

"What kind of thing?" Oreste asked.

"I didn't get a good LOOK, but it seemed

like an old book. We didn't stop because we were in a **HURRY** to finish the competition, but I've been wondering whether it might have been something important."

"There's only one way to find out," Professor Angel said. "Let's

investigate first thing TOMORROW MORNING! What time is your FLIGHT back to Whale Island?"

"It's not until late AFTERNOON," Colette replied.

"Perfect!" squeaked the professor. "Then you can all come along!"

SEE YOU NEXT YEAR!

Bright and early the next morning, the Thea Sisters, Professor Angel, and Oreste found themselves in the library's basement archives.

"Is this the spot where we need to PUSH?" Nicky asked Violet.

"Yes," Violet explained. "We need to MOVE that stone slab to reveal the passageway Alessandro and I took to reach the courtyard."

Everyone worked together to move the stone.

"There it is!" Violet squeaked.

Oreste shined his flashlight at the spot where Violet was pointing, illuminating a dusty book.

"Wow!" Colette gasped in surprise. "You were right, Vi!"

"I told you!" Violet said, smiling.

Professor Angel picked up the book carefully as Oreste held the light.

"Hmmm," the professor said as she studied the volume.

"**Is it really old?**" Paulina asked.

"It is!" Professor Angel replied. "Violet, this is a truly *amazing* discovery!"

Violet smiled shyly.

"What do we do now?" Pam asked eagerly. "Do we bring it to the university?"

Oreste shook his head.

"We need to contact the local **archaeological superintendent**," he explained. "She will organize a study to determine the age of the book. Then it will be restored and preserved."

"What a find!" Professor Angel said happily. "This is a real **archaeological discovery**, and the five of you have been a big part of it. That doesn't happen *every day*!"

"It's been an honor," Nicky said. "But does anyone mind if we get going now? I'm a little **claustrophobic**!"

The others nodded and **headed** toward the exit. Once they were outside, Violet took out her cell phone and dialed a number.

"I want to call Alessandro," she told her friends. "He was there when I found the book."

Well done, mouselets!

Twenty minutes later, the Thea Sisters were sitting at a table in a **cafe** along with the students from Rome.

"I can't believe we **accidentally** found an ancient manuscript!" Alessandro squeaked when he heard the news.

"That's incredible."

"We didn't win the **competition**, but this is even better!" Flaminia added. "What an important discovery."

"I wish this wasn't the last year of the archaeology games," Colette said sadly. "It's such a shame."

At that moment, Violet's cell phone rang.

"Hello, Professor!" she said into her phone. For the next few minutes, Violet listened carefully.

"Hmm," Violet said. "Oh, really? Fantastic!"

As soon as Violet hung up the phone, her friends turned to her, eager for news.

"Well?" Colette asked. "Don't keep us in suspense, Vi!"

Her friend smiled.

"The superintendent confirmed that the book is authentic," Violet explained. "And

thanks to this discovery, the university will receive the funding Professor Angel needs to organize another **International Archaeology Games!**"

"Wow!" everyone exclaimed happily. "What great news!"

"And there's another **surprise**," Violet said. "Professor Angel invited us to return next year to present the prizes to the winners. So we'll see each other here in Rome again next year!"

The Thea Sisters and their new friends chattered happily for a while longer, but soon it was time to say good-bye.

"Until next year!" they squeaked as they gathered together in a huge hug!

♥ MICE TOGETHER, ♥
FRIENDS FOREVER! ♥

How wonderful!

We'll see each other next year!